Little green BOOKS ™

THE ADVENTURES OF an ALUMINUM Can

a STORY ABOUT RECYCLING

BY
alison inches

illustrated by
mark chambers

Then, *KABOOM!* A huge dynamite blast blew up my home—and me along with it! The rock where I lived was crushed into small pieces and loaded into railroad cars.

Now we're on our way to the PROCESSING PLANT. I'll miss it here, but I'm excited to see where they're taking me!

April 3

Hi, Diary!

Another doozy of a day! I got crushed and ground into a fine powder. After a bath I took a boat ride to a REFINERY. I like seeing and doing new things. Traveling is fun!

I'm in here (somewhere)!

Getting mixed with chemicals

Boat ride to the refinery

Can you find me here?

Here at the refinery, the machines hum, whir, and buzz all day. First the workers mixed me with chemicals. I felt fizzy inside and out! Then I turned into a mushy paste.

After a steam bath and a superhot oven dry, I became a beautiful white powder called ALUMINUM OXIDE.

April 8

Hello, Diary!

Today I had a chemical bath in a gigantic bathtub. They zapped me with electricity, and I turned red-hot!

Then they pumped me into a mold. When I came out, I was a long, rectangular sheet of aluminum.

Now I'm rolled up like a sleeping bag. I feel neat, tidy, and ready to go!

P.S. Diary, did you know aluminum is used to make bicycle frames, chewing gum wrappers, and even airplanes!

April 11
Hats off, Diary! I got my top today! That's like a hat for a can. It's made from a sheet of aluminum that gets fed through a press that stamps out thousands of tops every minute. But first . . .

I was stretched into the shape of a can and trimmed to just the right size.

After I was tested to make sure I had no holes, I was filled with delicious fruit.

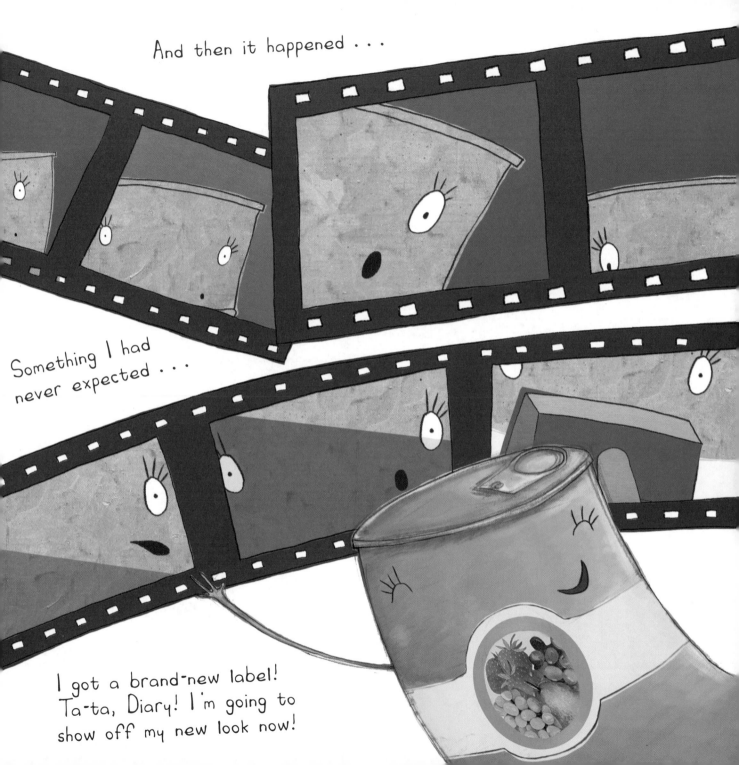

Wheeeeeeeeee!

May 14

Hi, Diary!

This past month at the MANUFACTURING PLANT and the fruit CANNERY sure has been a lot of fun!

Dressed in my fancy new label, I was put in a box with five other cans of fruit.

We were put in a truck and driven to a grocery store.

I wasn't on the store shelf for long before a nice lady scooped me up.

Guess where she took me next?

TO THE PARK! I saw the greenest trees and the bluest sky I'd ever seen.

Best of all, I saw my first baseball game!

A girl with braids hit a home run and won the game. It was so exciting!

When the game was over, the girl chose ME and celebrated as she ate the fruit. She said I was the best can of fruit ever. I love being an aluminum can!

It was really fun until the ants came along and tickled me. The little girl's mom didn't like the ants either, so she put me in the recycling bin.

Being a trophy was fun, but I was glad to get away from the ants. Hmmm, I wonder what's in store for me now?

I was taken to a SORTING PLANT, where I was separated from the glass and plastic, and then squashed into a BALE wth other aluminum cans. Then our bale was taken to the aluminum RECYCLING PLANT, where we were cleaned . . .

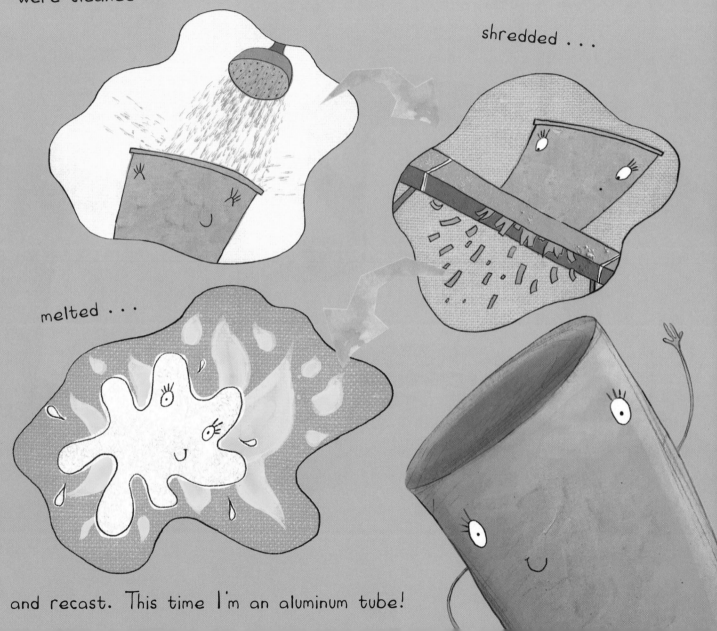

shredded . . .

melted . . .

and recast. This time I'm an aluminum tube!

June 1

Hold on to your pages, Diary! I've got BIG news! Today I got shipped to a baseball bat factory. I got made into a brand-new aluminum bat! Here's what happened:

They squeezed me through a mold and spun me round and round.

I got really dizzy! But all that spinning gave me a perfect shape.

Then I got a hot, salty bath and a heat treatment.

After that my ends were closed.
No more peeking inside me!

Later in the day, a knob and nonskid wrapping were added to my handle. Now I won't slip out of a baseball player's hands.

My favorite part of the day was when they shined me up and printed fun pictures and letters on my sides. I'm going to be the best bat ever!

June 30

Big news, Diary!

After I was packed, I was shipped to a sporting goods store. I stood straight and tall so everyone could see me.

That afternoon a boy named Robbie spotted me on the shelf.

He turned me over and smiled. "This is the one," he whispered. I felt so proud.

Tomorrow I'll be playing in my first baseball game! And guess what? It's a championship game! I'm going to try my best to make Robbie proud!

July 1
Home run, Diary! What a day! The bases were loaded and Robbie and I were at bat. He whispered, "Let's do it!" Then, PING! Robbie got the winning hit! Fans jumped out of their seats and cheered.

After Robbie rounded the bases, he picked me up and held me close. Now the fans were cheering for BOTH of us! I hope I don't get recycled for a long time.

NEW WORDS FROM THE ALUMINUM CAN'S DIARY

ALUMINUM OXIDE: a white powder that looks like table salt and is melted to make aluminum

BALE: a large bundle of the same items that are usually tied together so that they are easier to move

BAUXITE: any kind of rock that contains aluminum oxide, the powder used to make aluminum

CANNERY: a factory where cans are filled with things like fruit, vegetables, and tuna fish, and then sealed and labeled

MANUFACTURING PLANT: a factory that takes parts and supplies such as aluminum sheets and turns them into other items that can be sold or used, like aluminum cans

PROCESSING PLANT: a factory where natural things like rocks are put through chemicals and machines to turn them into something people can use

RECYCLING PLANT: a factory that takes items like plastic bottles, newspapers, and aluminum cans and turns them into new things that are usable

REFINERY: a factory where materials like bauxite are cleaned and treated to make things like aluminum sheets

SORTING PLANT: a place where recyclable objects like aluminum cans, glass bottles, and plastic containers are taken to be sorted and sent to the correct recycling plant